THE
PORRIDGE-POT
GOBLIN

by Jacqueline Jules
Illustrated by Hector Borlasca

To my editors at Apples & Honey Press
—JJ

To Mela Bolinao, my friend and agent
—HB

Apples & Honey Press
An Imprint of Behrman House Publishers
Millburn, New Jersey 07041

Text copyright © 2022 by Jacqueline Jules
Illustrations copyright © 2022 by Apples & Honey Press
ISBN 978-1-68115-591-3

Library of Congress Cataloging-in-Publication Data

Names: Jules, Jacqueline, 1956- author. | Borlasca, Hector, illustrator.
Title: The porridge pot goblin / by Jacqueline Jules ;
illustrated by Hector Borlasca.
Description: Millburn, New Jersey : Apples & Honey Press, [2022]
| Summary: "A pair of siblings must contend with an invisible goblin
as they prepare for Shabbat"-- Provided by publisher.
Identifiers: LCCN 2021031578 | ISBN 9781681155913 (hardcover)
Subjects: CYAC: Goblins--Fiction. | Jews--Fiction. | LCGFT: Picture books.
Classification: LCC PZ7.J92947 Po 2022 | DDC [E]--dc23
LC record available at https://lccn.loc.gov/2021031578

Design by Elynn Cohen
Edited by Ann D. Koffsky
Printed in China

1 3 5 7 9 8 6 4 2

Rose and Benny were braiding challah for Shabbat when they heard a rumbling noise outside.

"WHAT WAS THAT?" Benny asked.

"Shh!" Rose warned. "Mama is sleeping."

Mama was exhausted. She had been up all night helping mothers with their babies. That was her job, and the people in the village depended on her.

"Let Mama rest," Rose said. "We'll see what's wrong."

"How did this happen?" Rose asked.

"A goblin!" Benny said.

"Don't be silly," Rose answered.

"Look!" Benny pointed. "Tracks!"

Everyone in the village knew about goblins. Their bodies were invisible. But their rooster-like feet left prints.

"Where do they go?" Rose examined the ground.

"Maybe we should follow them," Benny said.

"All right," Rose agreed. "But we have to be back soon. There's a lot to do before Shabbat."

WHOOSH!

The children followed the three-toed tracks across the muddy field to an old oak.

Rose put her hands on her cheeks. "This knothole is as big as our porridge pot!"
"The goblin must live here," Benny said.

A smoky wind swirled out of the knothole and knocked the cap off Benny's head. Rose and Benny ran home without looking back.

Inside the cottage, Benny panted. "Are we safe?"
"I hope so." Rose shivered.

They washed their hands and went back to braiding the challah. All was quiet.

UNTIL...

Rose felt a tug on her hair.
She whirled around. Benny did too.

YANK! Rose's kerchief flew off her head. The
red cloth swirled through the room and up the chimney.

"It's the **GOBLIN!**"

Benny dove under the kitchen table.
Rose joined him.

"The kiddush cup, the candlesticks,"
Benny worried. "We need them
for Shabbat."

CLANG!

Nothing was damaged, but the noise woke Mama.

"What's going on?" she called downstairs in a sleepy voice.

"It's all right, Mama!" Rose called back. "We'll take care of it."

Rose took Benny's hand. "Let's talk outside."

"The goblin has to go!" Rose declared.

Benny nodded. "He'll ruin Shabbat!"

They both shuddered, imagining the candles blown out, the kiddush cup toppled, the challah cover flying up the chimney.

"How do we stop him?" Benny cried. "If he lives in that knothole in the tree, he could be as big as our porridge pot!"

"But not bigger," Rose suddenly realized. "I have a plan."

They tiptoed back into the house. Rose sprinkled flour on the floor.

"What are you doing?" asked Benny.

"You'll see," said Rose.

"I'm afraid," Benny whispered.

"Me too." Rose hugged him.

They crouched in a corner to wait.

Soon after, footprints appeared on the floured floor.
Rose leapt out, holding the porridge pot high.

BAM! She slammed it over the tracks.
The goblin was trapped!
But not for long...

The pot rose and ran around the kitchen on white-floured feet.

"Uh-oh!" Benny whispered.

Stuck under the pot, the goblin knocked into one thing after another. BUMP! BUMP! BUMP!

The goblin struggled, shaking the pot back and forth in the air.

Rose and Benny inched forward, gathering courage.
"NOW!" Rose lunged.
Together, they were heavy enough to stop the wiggling
pot from turning over.

A squeaky voice whined, "Please let me go home!"

Benny looked at Rose. She nodded.

They slid the pot across the kitchen and gently tipped it out the door.

"Don't come back!" Rose warned.

"I won't!" The goblin squeaked. "Your house is no fun!"

Rose and Benny
watched floury white
tracks race across the field.
"We did it!" Benny
cheered.

"Now let's finish getting ready
for Shabbat," Rose said.

Mama woke from her long nap, refreshed and rested. The family had a peaceful dinner, enjoying delicious challah and matzah ball soup. The Shabbat candles glowed undisturbed.

Benny looked over at the porridge pot, cleaned and by the hearth. He smiled at Rose. They were ready if the goblin ever came back.

Dear Readers,

Did you know that Jewish folklore includes stories of invisible goblins? The rabbis of the Talmud suggested sprinkling ashes on the floor to reveal the goblins' footprints, which looked just like a rooster's.

In this story, a goblin arrives on Friday morning—just as Benny and Rose are looking forward to Shabbat. Shabbat begins each Friday night, when candles are lit, followed by blessings made over a cup of wine and braided challah bread. It is a treasured day of peace and prayer, and certainly NOT a good time to have a mischievous goblin in the house!

Benny and Rose didn't know if they had the courage to capture a goblin. But they were determined to save Shabbat and restore peace to their home. Sometimes, when we are faced with a tough challenge and find a way to overcome it, we discover that we are much stronger than we think.

Wishing you peaceful Shabbats and happy family times.